A HORSE FOR CHRISTMAS

A HORSE FOR CHRISTMAS

ERIC HENDERSHOT

SWEETWATER BOOKS
AN IMPRINT OF CEDAR FORT, INC.
SPRINGVILLE, UTAH

ISBN 13: 978-1-4621-1078-0

Published by Sweetwater Books, an imprint of Cedar Fort, Inc., 2373 W. 700 S., Springville, UT 84663
Distributed by Cedar Fort, Inc., www.cedarfort.com

LIBRARY OF CONGRESS CATALOGING-IN-PUBLICATION DATA

Hendershot, Eric, author.
  A horse for Christmas / Eric Hendershot.
     pages cm
  Summary: After watching a movie about the wild mustangs of Nevada, fourth-graders Stoney and Tyler and Tyler's nosy little sister Sam follow their dream of capturing a mustang of their own by stowing away in a Jeep headed to Nevada.
  ISBN 978-1-4621-1078-0 (alk. paper)
  1. Christmas stories, American. [1. Mustang--Fiction. 2. Horses--Fiction. 3. Nevada--Fiction. 4. Friendship--Fiction. 5. Brothers and sisters--Fiction. 6. Voyages and travels--Fiction. 7. Christmas--Fiction.] I. Title.

  PZ7.H3786Hor 2012
  [Fic]--dc23
                              2012026275

Cover design by Brian Halley
Cover design © 2012 by Lyle Mortimer
Edited and typeset by Michelle Stoll

Printed in the United States of America

10 9 8 7 6 5 4 3 2 1

Acknowledgment

Dear readers,

This book is dedicated to all the horse-crazy boys and girls in the world but especially to my horse-crazy father, Claude Hendershot. He is, without a doubt, the inspiration for this book.

No one loved horses more than my father did. Whenever we would go on a trip, it always took us twice as long to get to our destination, because he had to stop and look at every horse along the way. No kidding, *every* horse! When he was just a young boy, he began drawing horses. He served in World War II, and when the war ended he went to art school, where he learned to draw horses even better.

I can still see him talking on the phone, doodling and sketching horses in the margins of the newspaper. Then he began doing oil paintings. He was really good—

so good, in fact, that he would take his paintings to horse farms and trade one of his paintings for a real horse. At one time, we had four horses in our garage! I have included one of his sketches. I hope you enjoy it.

—Eric Hendershot

Contents

Chapter 1

Wild Mustangs

Mrs. Smith stood in front of her fourth grade class and announced, "Students, today we are going to watch a film called *The Wild Mustangs of Nevada*."

It was at that very moment that Tyler Rogers's crazy wild-horse adventure began.

Everyone knew that Tyler was horse-crazy. That's all he ever talked about or dreamed about. He loved horses more than anything in the whole wide world. On his birthday, before he blew out the candles, his wish was always to have a horse of his very own. When he grew up, his plan was to own a big horse ranch with open fields and big barns full of horses—all kinds of horses, like thoroughbreds, Arabians, Appaloosas, saddlebreds, quarter horses, pintos, palominos, and every other kind of horse he could think of.

Every Christmas since he could remember, he would ask for a real live horse. His conversation with his mom always went something like this:

"Tyler," his mother would say, "what would you like for Christmas this year?"

"A horse."

"We don't have any place to keep a horse."

"Yes, we do. We can keep it in the garage."

"There's no room in the garage."

"There's lots of room in the garage, if Dad would just park his truck in the driveway!"

That's when his mother would shake her head, roll her eyes, and say, "The neighbors wouldn't like it, and besides, our neighborhood isn't zoned for horses."

"What does 'zoned' mean?"

"It means the city won't let you have horses in your garage."

"What about dogs? The city lets people have dogs, don't they?"

"Dogs are different. They're not as big as horses."

"Oh yeah. Well, what about Jake Hansen's Great

Dane, Goliath? Every time Jake walks by with Goliath, Dad says, 'Look at the size of that dog! He's as big as a horse!'"

Right about then, Tyler's mom would give Tyler *the look* and say, "Tyler, ask for something else besides a horse because you are *not* getting a horse for Christmas! And I don't want to hear about it again!"

Even after his mom said that, he still kept asking for a horse.

Anyway, Tyler thought the movie was awesome! He learned that Spanish *conquistadors* (conquerors) brought horses to the new world in search of gold. They raised their horses on ranches in New Mexico. Some of these horses escaped and ran free. The free running ones were called "mustangs." The word "mustang" comes from the Spanish word *mestano*, which means "stray" or "free-running animal." He also learned that there are over thirty thousand of these wild mustangs running free in Nevada! Thirty thousand! The thought of this made Tyler wild with excitement.

As soon as the bell rang to go home, Tyler hurried to the front of the room, where Mrs. Smith was cleaning off the white board, and said, "Mrs. Smith, in the movie they said there are thirty thousand wild mustangs running free."

"That's correct," said Mrs. Smith.

"Does anybody own them?" asked Tyler.

"Nobody owns them," said Mrs. Smith.

Tyler couldn't believe it. He could hardly go to sleep that night. All he could think about was going to Nevada and catching one of those wild mustangs. And when he finally did fall asleep, he had the coolest dream. He dreamed he was riding bareback across the desert on a beautiful white stallion. It was like he was flying. The stallion's hooves, pounding the desert floor, sounded like thunder. The wind whistled in his ears and blew the horse's long, white mane into Tyler's face, tickling his nose.

But then the dream turned into a nightmare when his little sister, Sam, showed up in the dream. She was just a year younger than Tyler but acted like she was his mother. At least that's what Tyler thought. There she was, with her perfect little pigtails, acting all disgusted with her hands on her hips, shaking her head and rolling her big brown eyes. She always acted like this when she talked to Tyler. "She's such a little know-it-all," Tyler would tell his friends.

"TYLER!" she shouted real loud.

"Whoa!" said Tyler, pulling back hard on the reins. The big horse stopped right in front of Sam.

"What?" said Tyler, looking down at Sam.

"Get off that horse and get dressed or you're gonna miss the bus!"

Tyler was confused. "What?" he said again. And then he woke from his dream.

There was Sam, standing right next to his bed with her hands on her hips, shaking her head just like in the dream.

"What'd you say?" asked Tyler, still half asleep.

"I said, get off that horse and get dressed or you're gonna miss the bus!"

"Wait a minute! How'd you know I was dreaming about riding a horse?"

"'Cause that's all you *ever* dream about. Now get up!" Then she turned and walked out of the room.

It was a good thing Sam woke Tyler up when she did, because he almost did miss the bus.

Chapter 2

Stoney Davis

The day before Christmas vacation, Mrs. Smith introduced a new student to the class. "Boys and girls," she said. "We have a new student who just moved here. Stoney, please come up and tell the class a little bit about yourself."

The whole class watched as Stoney got up from his seat and walked slowly to the front of the room. He was short with skinny, bowed legs, and he was dressed just like a real cowboy. He wore a big white cowboy hat that almost covered his squinty blue eyes and had a colorful scarf tied around his neck. He had on a cool-looking leather vest and a pair of real leather chaps over his Wrangler jeans. He even had on cowboy boots and a real pair of silver spurs that jingled and jangled as he walked.

He was carrying a real calf-roping rope. When Stoney got to the front of the class, he turned, smiled, and said, "Howdy, everybody. My name's Stoney Davis, and I'm from the great state of Texas! Down in Texas, I lived on a big ranch with a thousand head of cattle." Then he held up the rope and said, "This here's a rope we use for ropin' calves. Down in Texas we call calves 'little doggies.' Would you like to see how we rope little doggies?"

The whole class nodded and said, "Yes!"

"Okay," said Stoney. "Who's gonna be my little doggie?"

Everybody laughed, but no one raised their hand.

Then Stoney spotted Katelyn Johnson, the cutest girl in the class.

"How 'bout you? Do you wanna be my little doggie?"

Everybody laughed again, including Mrs. Smith.

Katelyn was so embarrassed that her face turned all red as she walked up the aisle to the front of the class.

"Okay, little doggie," said Stoney to Katelyn. "Start running."

Katelyn took off running around the classroom with Stoney right behind her. Everybody was cheering and laughing. Then, just as Katelyn reached the front of the room, Stoney twirled his rope in the air and sent it flying. It was perfect! It went right over Katelyn's head and shoulders and slipped down around her waist. Stoney yanked on the rope. The rope tightened, and Katelyn came to a stop.

"And that's how we rope little doggies!" said Stoney.

The whole class thought it was really cool and clapped.

After watching Stoney lasso Katelyn, Tyler started thinking. If he ever figured out how to get to Nevada to catch a wild mustang, Stoney would be the one to take with him. So at recess, Tyler made sure he got Stoney's phone number.

Well, you'll never guess what happened later that day. When Tyler came home from school, his big brother, Brad, was in the kitchen packing a bunch of food into a cooler. Brad was home from college for Christmas vacation. Brad was Tyler's hero. Tyler thought Brad was the coolest, nicest big brother anybody could ever have. He always played basketball with Tyler and took him to fun places.

"Where's Mom?" asked Tyler.

"Shopping," said Brad. "She said she'd be home to fix dinner."

Tyler walked over to the counter, jumped up on it, and sat down.

"What are you doing?"

"Getting ready for my trip."

"What trip?"

"I'm going to see Jen."

"Who's Jen?"

"A girl I met at college."

"You're gonna be here for Christmas, aren't you?" asked Tyler, all worried.

"Oh, yeah," said Brad, "I'll only be gone for a couple of days."

"That's good," said Tyler.

Brad stuffed two sandwiches into the cooler.

"Is she cute?"

"I think so."

"Are you gonna marry her?"

Brad laughed as he crammed an apple into the cooler next to the sandwiches. "I don't know. Maybe someday."

"When are you leaving?"

"Five-thirty tomorrow morning."

"Where does Jen live?"

"A little town called Lewis."

"Where's Lewis?"

"In Nevada."

NEVADA! When Brad said "Nevada," Tyler almost fell off the counter. He couldn't believe it. Brad was going to Nevada, where all the wild Mustangs were!

Tyler wondered if it was meant to be. Maybe at last he was finally going to get a horse of his very own for Christmas!

That night, he snuck into the living room, hid behind the Christmas tree, and called Stoney on his mom's cell phone. He told Stoney all about Brad going to Nevada and asked him if he wanted to come along and catch a wild mustang. When Stoney said he did, Tyler told him to bring all of his ropes and to be at Tyler's house twenty minutes after five the next morning.

When Tyler went to bed that night, he set his alarm for five o'clock and then put it under his pillow so no one could hear it when it went off.

Chapter 3

Nevada!

Before Tyler knew it, the alarm went off! He got dressed real fast and snuck up the stairs as quietly as he could. He knew horses really liked carrots, so he took all the carrots out of the fridge and put them into a bag. Then he wrote his mom and dad a quick note that said—

Dear Mom and Dad,

    I'll be back for dinner with a BIG surprise.

Love,
Tyler

He put the note on the refrigerator with a magnet. Then he went into the garage, crossed to the door that went into the backyard, and opened it. Stoney was waiting right outside, just like they planned.

"C'mon," said Tyler. "But be real quiet."

They quietly opened the back door of Brad's Jeep Cherokee, climbed over the backseat, and hid under a blanket. Just then, they heard the kitchen door open and somebody walking toward the jeep.

"Shhh!" Tyler said as quiet as he could. Tyler and Stoney looked at each other and held their breath. The car door opened, and all of sudden the blanket they were hiding under got ripped right off of them!

They looked up, expecting to see Brad, but instead they saw Sam! She was kneeling on the backseat staring at them. "What do you think you're doing?" asked Sam.

Tyler didn't want to tell her that they were going to Nevada to catch wild mustangs, so he just said, "Nothing."

"Don't lie to me, Tyler," she said. "I know what you're doing."

"What?" said Tyler.

"You're going to Nevada to catch a wild mustang."

Stoney and Tyler just looked at each other, wondering how she knew.

"How'd you know that?" asked Tyler.

"I heard you talking on the phone last night behind the Christmas tree," she said. "And I'm coming too!"

"No, you're not!" said Tyler.

"Fine," said Sam. "But if I can't come, I'm gonna go and tell Mom and Dad what you're doing!"

Just then they heard the kitchen door open.

Sam panicked and said, "Brad's coming!"

Tyler and Stoney had no choice but to take Sam with them.

"Hurry!" said Tyler. "Quick! Get under the blanket!"

Sam dove into the back and crawled under the blanket with Tyler and Stoney.

"You'll be glad I came," whispered Sam.

Tyler just shook his head and rolled his eyes.

Brad got into the jeep and started the engine. They could hear the garage door open, and before they knew it, they were on their way to Nevada!

It seemed like they were under the blanket forever. All they could hear were the tires humming on the road and music from Brad's radio.

"I've gotta go to the bathroom," whispered Tyler.

"Me too," said Stoney.

Sam rolled her eyes and shook her head. "Why didn't you both go before we came?"

Just then, they felt the car go off the road, slow down, and finally stop.

"I wonder why Brad's stopping," said Tyler.

"Maybe we're there," said Sam.

"I don't think so," said Tyler.

"Maybe he has to go to the bathroom too," said Stoney.

"He's probably stopping to get gas," said Sam.

Then they heard Brad's door open and close.

"I'll look and see," said Tyler.

"Don't let him see you!" said Sam.

"Don't worry. I won't."

Tyler slowly lifted the blanket off his head and peeked out the back window. They were at a gas station all right, and Tyler could see Brad going inside the station to pay.

"You were right, Stoney. Brad's getting gas."

"I really gotta go to the bathroom," said Stoney.

"Me too!" said Tyler. "C'mon, let's go!"

All three of the kids threw off the blanket, climbed over the backseat, opened the door, and ran as fast as they could to the restrooms. Luckily for them, the restrooms were outside, so they didn't have to go inside the station where Brad was.

Just when Sam came out of the women's restroom, she saw Brad come out of the station. He was heading right toward her! She didn't have anywhere to hide, so she quickly covered her head with her jacket and walked right by him! Luckily, Brad never guessed it was her.

Sam hurried back to the jeep, climbed in, and hid

under the blanket again. As she waited for Tyler and Stoney, she heard a man talking to someone on his cell phone.

"Don't you worry 'bout nothin', Ray," Sam heard him say. "This ain't our first rodeo. We know how to *steal* a horse! You just worry 'bout gettin' us the money when we get that stallion."

Sam pulled off the blanket and peeked out of the side window just in time to get a quick look at the man. He was at the next gas pump, filling up an old, beat-up pickup truck. He was tall and skinny with long scraggly hair and a black patch over his right eye.

"We'll be talking soon, Ray," Sam heard him say. Then he turned off his cell phone, got into the pickup truck, and drove off. Sam noticed that the truck had a horse trailer with two horses inside hooked to it.

Meanwhile, when Stoney and Tyler opened the door to leave the restroom, they got a big surprise—Brad was standing right outside waiting to come in! They quickly closed the door and locked it real fast. It was a good thing for them that Brad wasn't looking their way because he would have seen them for sure.

Inside the restroom, Tyler and Stoney stood motionless and stared at each other for a long time. Their hearts were really thumping.

"What are we gonna do now?" asked Stoney. "If we go out there, he's gonna see us."

"I don't know," whispered Tyler

Then Tyler got an idea!

"Quick, Stoney! Get me a bunch of toilet paper."

"What for?"

"You'll see."

Stoney hurried to the toilet paper, grabbed a big bunch, and handed it to Tyler.

"Now give me your hat," said Tyler.

Stoney took off his hat and handed it to Tyler.

"Okay," said Tyler quietly. "Here's what we're gonna do."

About a minute later, they opened the bathroom door, stepped out, and walked right past Brad. Brad never guessed it was Tyler and Stoney because Tyler was wearing Stoney's big cowboy hat way down over his eyes and had a big bunch of toilet paper over his face pretending to blow his nose. Of course Brad didn't know who Stoney was because he had never seen Stoney before. Tyler's idea worked! Just as soon as Brad went into the restroom, Tyler and Stoney ran as fast as they could back to the jeep.

Chapter 4
The General

Before long, they were on the road again. They had been traveling for about an hour when, all of a sudden, Tyler, Stoney, and Sam heard a *thumping* sound coming from under the hood of the jeep. Brad put on the brakes, slowed down, and pulled off the road.

"I wonder what's wrong," whispered Stoney.

They could hear Brad turn off the engine and get out of the jeep. Then they heard him open the hood.

"I'll take a look," said Tyler.

"*No, Tyler!*" said Sam. "He'll see you!"

"Relax. I'll be real careful."

Tyler slowly lifted off the blanket, got up on his knees, and looked out over the seats through the windshield. He couldn't see Brad because the hood was up. He looked out the side windows and could see that they were in the middle of nowhere. For miles and miles, all he could see was desert and sagebrush. And then, all of a sudden, Brad closed the hood. Tyler quickly ducked back down and hid under the blanket.

"Did he see you?" asked Stoney.

"I don't know," said Tyler, all nervous-like.

"He saw you, didn't he?" said Sam, all upset.

Brad did see something, but he wasn't sure what it was. He walked slowly to the back of the jeep looking in the side windows. Then he opened the hatch, reached in, and yanked the blanket off Tyler, Stoney, and Sam!

Brad couldn't believe his eyes when he saw the three of them lying in the back looking up at him.

"Hi," said Sam.

"Hi," said Tyler

"Howdy," said Stoney.

Brad's eyes got pitch black, just the way his dad's did the day Tyler hit the golf ball in the family room and broke the big aquarium, sending the water and tropical fish splashing all over the carpet.

"Get out of there right now!" shouted Brad.

Tyler, Stoney, and Sam slid out of the back and stared helplessly up at Brad.

"*What are you doing here?*" shouted Brad.

Stoney and Sam looked at Tyler.

"This was your idea," said Sam. "Tell him."

Tyler looked up at Brad and said, "We were gonna catch a wild mustang."

"A wild mustang? What! Are you kidding me, Tyler?" shouted Brad.

Tyler didn't know what to say, so he didn't say anything.

"You guys are gonna be in big trouble with Mom and Dad! You know that, don't you? Now get in the car!"

Brad opened the back door and, one by one, Tyler, Stoney, and Sam got in.

"Lock the doors and stay here and don't move!" said Brad. "I have to go back to that station and get a new fan belt. And *then* we're going home! "

Brad took his cell phone out of his pocket and handed it to Tyler. "Take this. I'll call you when I get to the station."

"Brad?" asked Tyler.

"What?"

"Are we in Nevada?"

"Yes, we're in Nevada! We've been in Nevada for an hour."

Just then, coming from the other direction, they saw a real nice truck pulling the biggest and nicest horse trailer any of them had ever seen. It slowed to a stop on the other side of the road. On the side of the horse trailer was printed, in great big gold and black letters, "THE GENERAL—HORSE OF THE YEAR."

The driver of the truck was an older man with gray hair and a beard. He wore glasses and a white cowboy hat. Sitting next to him was his granddaughter. She was a pretty girl about Brad's age. She was tall and thin and had long brown hair and dark brown eyes.

The driver rolled down his window and asked, "Having trouble?"

"Yeah," said Brad holding up the broken fan belt, "I've gotta get a new one of these."

"I'm JP MacDonald, and this is my granddaughter Andi."

"It's nice to meet you. My name's Brad Rogers."

JP looked at Andi and said with a smile, "What do you think, Andi? Can we trust him?"

Andi looked at Brad and smiled.

"I think so," said Andi. "He looks pretty harmless."

"Okay, young man," said JP. "Climb in."

"Thanks a lot. I really appreciate this," said Brad. Brad ran around the front of the truck, opened the door, and slid in next to Andi.

Chapter 5

A Mustang for Brad

Tyler, Stoney, and Sam sat in the backseat and waited and waited for Brad to come back. To kill time, Sam and Stoney played rock-paper-scissors. Tyler was staring out the window at a hill about a mile away.

Finally he said, "Hey, you guys. See that hill over there? Let's just walk over to it and see if maybe there are some horses behind it."

Sam and Stoney stopped playing and looked past Tyler to the hill. Sam started shaking her head and said, "Tyler, you heard what Brad said. We're supposed to stay right here!"

"I know," said Tyler. "But what if there's a whole herd of wild mustangs on the other side of that hill?"

Stoney and Sam leaned forward and looked at the hill again.

"Stoney," said Tyler, "if you could pick any horse, what color would you want him to be?"

Stoney thought about it for a minute and then said, "A black and white pinto stallion."

"How 'bout you, Sam?" asked Tyler.

It didn't take any time at all for Sam to answer. "Pure white, like the snow," she said.

Then Stoney asked Tyler what he would pick.

"That's easy," said Tyler. "A chestnut-brown stallion with a black mane and tail and a white star on his forehead."

There was a long moment of silence as they all stared off thinking and dreaming about a horse of their very own.

"This place," said Tyler, looking out the window, "looks just like the movie we saw in class, where all the wild horses were. I betcha a gazillion dollars there's a herd of wild mustangs out there, somewhere, just waiting for us."

"Tyler," said Sam. "I know what you're thinking, but we have to stay right here, or Brad's gonna be real mad."

That's when Tyler got a great idea. "He wouldn't be mad if we got him a wild mustang too. Would he?" asked Tyler.

Sam didn't say anything, but Tyler could tell she agreed. Tyler leaned forward, grabbed a piece of paper and a pen out of the glove box, and began writing a note to Brad.

"What are you doing?" asked Sam.

"I'm writing a note to Brad."

Sam folded her arms and said, "I don't think this is a good idea, Tyler."

"Don't worry. If there aren't any horses on the other side of that hill, we'll come right back."

Tyler finished the note and put it on Brad's seat, right where he could find it.

"C'mon, let's go!" said Tyler as he opened the door.

They all got out of the jeep and started walking across the desert toward the hill. They were so excited they could hardly stand it.

The hill was a lot farther away and a lot steeper than it looked from Brad's jeep. When they finally got to the top of the hill, they couldn't see any mustangs on the other side.

"Okay," said Sam. "No mustangs. Let's go back."

Tyler looked back at the jeep and said, "Brad's not even back yet. Let's just go to that other hill over there and take a look. If there aren't any mustangs there, I promise we'll go back."

"Tyler!" said Sam, just the way her mom said it when she wanted Tyler to do something he didn't want to do. "I think we should go back *now*!"

"If you wanna go back to the car, Sam," said Tyler, "go ahead. But me and Stoney are going over to that hill! C'mon, Stoney."

Tyler started down the other side of the hill with Stoney right behind him. Sam hesitated for a second, then shouted, "Hey, wait for me!" Then she ran down the hill after them.

Meanwhile, Andi and her grandpa brought Brad back to the jeep, said good-bye, then turned around and headed for their ranch. When Brad opened the car door and saw that Tyler, Stoney, and Sam were gone, he was really worried. Then when he found the note Tyler had written, he was upset.

Dear Brad,

Don't worry because we're gonna get you a wild mustang too.

Love,

Tyler

After he read it, he crumpled it up into a ball, threw it into the backseat, and slammed the door.

"Tyler! *Tyler!*" he yelled as loud as he could in all directions. But there was no answer. He had no idea where to look. Then he remembered that he had given Tyler his cell phone. He would fix the car as fast as he could then drive back to the station and call Tyler from the station's pay phone. He lifted the jeep's hood and went to work.

Chapter 6

Horse of the Year

Luke Dawson was the name of the tall, skinny guy with the scraggly hair and the patch over his eye who Sam saw and heard at the gas station. Luke and his cousin Karl were notorious horse thieves and were getting ready to steal The General and sell him. The General was worth a lot of money because he had just won the "Horse of the Year" award for the fifth straight year!

They pulled their truck and horse trailer to the side of the road and waited for JP and Andi to come along.

When JP's truck got close, Luke stepped to the middle of the road and started waving his arms for JP to stop and give him some help. Karl was hiding behind the horse trailer. As soon as JP saw Luke, he pulled to the side of the road and rolled down his window.

"Need some help?" asked JP.

"'Fraid so," said Luke. "You know anything 'bout cars?"

"Enough to get myself in trouble," said JP, chuckling. JP and Andi got out of the truck and walked with Luke toward Luke and Karl's truck.

"I sure do appreciate this," said Luke.

"Glad we can help," said JP.

Then, just as they passed the horse trailer, Karl jumped out and grabbed Andi from behind and held her tight! Andi screamed and shouted,"GRANDPA! HELP!"

JP turned to look back, but Luke spun him around and shoved him up against the trailer.

"Hey!" shouted JP. "Let go of her!"

Luke grabbed hold of JP's jacket and pulled him in so close they were nose to nose. "We ain't gonna hurt nobody!" shouted Luke. "All's we're after is the *horse*!"

JP and Andi looked at each other.

"No!" shouted Andi. "You can't have The General!"

"C'mon," said Luke. "Let's tie these two up!"

The two men dragged JP and Andi to the other

side of the trailer, pushed them to the ground, and tied their hands behind their backs.

JP and Andi watched helplessly as Karl walked back to their horse trailer, swung open the doors, and led The General out. The big horse was excited to be out of the trailer. He threw his head back, whinnied, and pranced around.

"Whoa, boy. Easy now," said Karl nervously.

The General was one of the most beautiful horses in the whole wide world. He was a big, strong, brown and white pinto stallion with a bald face. "Bald face" means his face was all white.

"You're not gonna get away with this!" shouted JP.

"Be quiet, old man!" shouted Luke.

Just as Karl was about to put The General into their trailer, Andi shouted out. "Go, Gen! *Go!*"

At the sound of Andi's voice, The General immediately reared up on his hind legs.

"Go, Gen!" Andi shouted again.

"Be quiet!" shouted Luke.

But Andi didn't listen and kept right on shouting, "Go, Gen! *Go!*"

By this time, Karl was white with fear as he used all his strength trying to control The General.

"Easy, boy! Easy!" Karl kept repeating.

"Go, Gen! Run!" shouted Andi.

"Quiet!" shouted Luke.

The General's razor-sharp hooves were slashing in the air and coming real close to Karl's head. Karl backed away, slipped on some loose rocks, and fell. When he hit the ground, he was still holding onto the rope. But The General's bridle broke loose and fell right into Karl's lap. The General was free!

"Go, Gen! Go, Gen!" Andi kept shouting.

The General reared up again, then turned and galloped out across the desert.

"Get back here, you dumb horse!" shouted Karl.

But there was no way The General was coming back.

"We gotta get him!" shouted Luke. "C'mon, let's go!"

Luke and Karl ran back to their truck, jumped in, and drove off in a cloud of dust, leaving JP and Andi tied up behind the trailer.

Meanwhile, as Brad was hurrying back to the station, he spotted JP's truck and trailer on the side of the road. Thinking they had broken down and needed help, he stopped. When he didn't see them in the cab, he walked around to the other side of the trailer, where he found them tied up. After Brad finished untying them, they all drove back to the station and called the sheriff. When the sheriff showed up, JP told him everything that had happened.

Brad tried to call Tyler on his cell phone, but Tyler

had it turned off because he was afraid it might spook the wild mustangs.

At this point, Brad was desperate. He told Andi the whole story of how Tyler, Stoney, and Sam hid under the blanket and were now somewhere in the desert looking for wild mustangs.

"So what are you gonna do?" asked Andi.

"There's only one thing to do—I've gotta find them."

"You can't go alone. It's too easy to get lost out there. I'll go with you if you want."

"Are you sure?"

"Yes."

"Thanks," said Brad. "That would be great."

Andi got permission from JP, then got in the jeep with Brad and raced back to find the kids.

Chapter 7

Peanut Butter and Jelly

When the kids didn't see mustangs on the other side of the second hill, they went to the third and then to the fourth.

Just then, Stoney did something strange. He took off his hat, dropped to his knees, and put his ear to the ground.

"What are you doing?" asked Tyler.

"Shhh!" he said. "I'm listening."

"For what?" said Tyler.

"For horses," he said. "Back in Texas, this is how we know where the cattle herds are."

Stoney listened for a little while longer, then got to his feet.

"What'd you hear?" asked Sam.

"Did you hear any horses?" asked Tyler.

"Nope, no horses," answered Stoney. "Just some jack rabbits and a desert turtle 'bout a mile away."

"There *aren't* any horses out here!" shouted Sam. "I think we should go back. *Now!*"

The last thing Tyler wanted to do was go back, but he didn't have a choice. "Okay, let's go back," he said.

So they started walking back. Tyler had no idea where they were going, but he couldn't tell Sam that. Everything looked the same. They walked for what

seemed like forever but still didn't see Brad's jeep or even a road.

Tyler didn't say anything to Stoney or Sam, but he was starting to get scared—real scared. He was having all kinds of scary thoughts. Like what if they starved to death and big, ugly bald-headed vultures flew out of the sky and ate all of their flesh right down to their bones? Or what if when it got dark, a bunch of hungry coyotes attacked them? Or what if they fell asleep and poisonous scorpions crawled up their pants and stung them on their legs? Or what if they walked into a nest of rattlesnakes that bit them to death? Then he pictured his mom on the TV news crying and pleading with people not to give up looking for them. He made a promise, right there and then, that if he ever made it back to California alive, the first thing he was gonna do was go right in and tell Mrs. Smith that the movie about the wild mustangs of Nevada was just a big bunch of baloney.

When they got to the top of yet another hill, all they could see was more desert. That's when Sam started to cry.

"We're lost, Tyler!" she shouted. "Don't you know that? It wasn't this far back to the jeep! What are we gonna do?"

"Don't worry. We'll find Brad's jeep," said Tyler.

"*Where?*" she shouted. Then she started pointing. "Brad's jeep could be that way, or that way, or that way!"

Just then, Tyler heard a noise. At first he thought it was thunder. But it couldn't be thunder because there wasn't one cloud in the entire sky. The noise was coming from behind them and was getting louder and louder. They all turned to see what it was, and there in front of them, running across the desert, was the most beautiful horse they had ever seen. Of course, there was no way they could know that this beautiful horse was really The General. He was so beautiful that they thought he must be the king of all the wild mustangs! His nostrils were flared, his tail was standing up, and his mane was streaming in the wind. He raced right by them to the top of the hill, where he stopped, reared up on his hind legs, and whinnied. It was the awesomest thing Tyler, Stoney, and Sam had ever seen. With the blue sky behind him and his long mane blowing in the wind, it was just like a something out of a movie. Then he galloped back down the hill, stopped again, and started munching on some desert grass.

"Holy smokes!" said Tyler. "We're gonna catch us a wild mustang after all!"

"How are we gonna do that?" asked Stoney.

Tyler walked over to Stoney, put his hands on Stoney's shoulders, and said, "You're gonna take your rope and lasso him! And then we're gonna help you hold him!"

Stoney looked scared and just stared at Tyler for a long time.

"Well, what are you waiting for?" asked Tyler.

"I can't do it," said Stoney.

"What do you mean you can't do it?" Tyler asked.

Then Stoney did something that surprised Tyler. He looked down at the ground and said quietly, "I'm scared."

"You're scared? You're kidding, right? You've roped lots of horses. Right?"

Stoney just kept looking down at the ground, shaking his head.

Tyler couldn't believe it. "Well, fine then," he said. "I'll just have to rope him myself!"

Tyler grabbed the rope from Stoney and marched out into the desert toward the stallion. He was scared too, but he knew this was maybe the only chance he'd ever get to rope a wild mustang. Then the weirdest thing happened. As he walked toward the horse, the horse didn't run. He just looked up at Tyler and then went right back to eating the grass. Tyler got the rope ready and threw it, but he missed by a mile! He tried again and again and again but just couldn't get the rope over the horse's head.

Sam and Stoney were hiding behind some sage brush, shouting, "You can do it, Tyler! You can do it!"

But Tyler couldn't and didn't. He was getting tired. The stallion was in no hurry to go anywhere, so Tyler decided to take a break. He hung the rope on a tree branch and slowly walked back to Sam and Stoney.

"Did you see that? I almost got him," said Tyler. "I just need a little rest, then I'll rope him and we'll ride him back to Brad's jeep."

"Is anybody hungry?" asked Stoney.

"I brought some carrots," said Tyler.

"That's all you brought?" asked Sam with her eyebrows raised real high.

"Yeah," said Tyler.

"Well, then, I guess it's a good thing I came," said Sam. She took off her backpack, set it down on the ground, reached inside, and took out three wrapped sandwiches, a thermos jug, and some paper cups.

"Whoa!" said Stoney, all excited when he saw the sandwiches.

"Would you like a peanut butter and jelly sandwich, Stoney?" asked Sam.

"Yeah!" he said, reaching for one.

"Well, you're not gonna get one like that. What's the *magic* word?"

"May I *please* have a sandwich?"

"That's more like it," said Sam. "Would you like smooth or crunchy?"

"Crunchy . . . Please."

Sam handed Stoney a sandwich.

He ripped the plastic bag open and took a huge bite.

"Stoney!" scolded Sam. "That's disgusting! Take smaller bites."

"But I'm hungry!" he said with a peanut butter and jelly mustache.

"That's no excuse. Even when you're hungry, you should still have good manners."

"Okay . . . sorry," said Stoney, as he took another, smaller bite.

Sam unwrapped another sandwich and took a bite.

"Hey!" said Tyler. "What about me?"

"First, tell me you're glad I came," said Sam.

Tyler really didn't want to say it, but he was so hungry that he had to. "I'm glad you came." he said.

"Say you're really, really, really glad I came."

"I'm really, really, really glad you came."

"Okay, here's your sandwich," said Sam.

"Thanks, Sam."

"Man! I think this is the best peanut butter and jelly sandwich I've ever had," Stoney said between bites.

"Thank you, Stoney, but please don't talk with your mouth full."

"Sorry."

"Would anyone like some milk?" asked Sam.

"Yes, please!" said Stoney and Tyler almost at the same time.

Sam poured milk into two paper cups and handed them to Tyler and Stoney.

"Stoney," said Tyler, "why were you so scared to rope the horse? You roped horses and little doggies in Texas. Didn't you?"

Stoney just stared down at the ground.

Sam took another bite of her sandwich, looked at Stoney for a long time, then said, "You didn't really rope horses and little doggies in Texas, did you, Stoney?"

Stoney looked at Sam for a long moment, then sadly shook his head.

"You tell fibs because you think kids will like you more. Don't you, Stoney?" asked Sam.

Stoney slowly nodded his head.

"Well," said Sam. "You don't have to tell fibs any- more 'cause we like you just the way you are."

"Are you really from Texas?" asked Tyler.

Stoney shook his head again.

"Then where are you from?"

After a long time, Stoney quietly answered, "I'm from Winnemucca, Nevada."

"Winnemucca!" said a surprised Tyler.

"Yeah."

"Well, where'd you get the ropes and all the cowboy stuff?" asked Tyler.

"At a garage sale."

Just then Sam whispered, "Tyler! Stoney! *Look!*"

Tyler and Stoney both turned and looked. They couldn't believe what they saw! The stallion had walked right up behind Sam, lowered his big bald faced head over Sam's shoulder, and was eating the peanut butter and jelly sandwich right out of her hand! They watched, still as can be, until he finished the sandwich and slowly walked away.

Now that they knew he liked peanut butter and jelly, they came up with a brand-new plan.

Chapter 8
Horse Thieves

Tyler, Stoney, and Sam walked real slow toward the stallion. Stoney was scared and held onto Sam's jacket. Tyler held the rope while Sam held out another peanut butter and jelly sandwich.

"Here horsey, nice horsey," she said. "Wanna 'nother bite?"

The stallion just stood there, watching them with his big brown eyes. Sam slowly raised the sandwich toward his mouth. And, just like they had planned and hoped, he lowered his head to take a bite.

"Okay, Sam," whispered Tyler. "Move your hand, and I'll put the rope over his head."

"No, Tyler," whispered Sam. "I think Stoney should do this."

"What?" said Stoney, all scared-like.

"Put the rope over his head, Stoney," ordered Sam.

"It's okay, Sam," said Stoney. "Tyler can do it."

"Stoney, you listen to me! Now! Take the rope and put it over the horse's head!"

"Do I have to?"

"Yes!"

The way Sam said it, Stoney knew she meant business. His hands were shaking as he took the rope from Tyler and carefully slipped it up and over the horse's head and ears. When the rope slipped down over the horse's neck, Stoney stepped back and tightened the loop.

"Stoney! You did it! You did it!" shouted Sam.

"Way to go Stoney!" said Tyler.

Stoney's face broke into a great big smile. "I did it!" he said, all excited. "I roped me a wild mustang!"

After they roped the horse, they named her Beauty.

It was Sam's idea. They couldn't decide if it was a he or a she, so they took a vote. Tyler thought it was a boy, but Sam and Stoney thought it was a girl, so that's how it got the name "Beauty." It wasn't until later that they found out that the horse was really a boy and his real name was The General.

They spent about an hour training him. It was

easy—so easy that they wished three more mustangs would come along so they could train them too. They were too short to get up on the horse's back, so they took turns getting on each other's shoulders and climbing on.

When they thought Beauty was trained real good, they headed back, hoping to find Brad's jeep. *Boy, is Brad gonna be surprised*, thought Tyler. He couldn't wait to show him their new horse.

After they had ridden Beauty for about a mile, they saw two men on horses riding toward them. It was Luke Dawson and his cousin Karl Dawson. They were looking for The General. Luke acted all friendly and nice, but Karl just looked at them real mean-like.

Luke got off his horse, walked over to the kids, and said, "I see you found our horse."

"What do you mean 'your horse'? He's a wild mustang. And he's ours," said Tyler.

"That's right," said Stoney. "I roped him myself."

"That's right," said Sam. "Beauty's ours."

Luke just laughed and shook his head. "As you can see, this ain't no wild horse, else you wouldn't be able to be ridin' him, now would ya? Ya see, a real wild mustang woulda bucked you off clear over yonder mountain."

"He *was* wild, but we trained him real good!" said Sam.

"That's right," said Stoney.

Tyler thought about what Luke said. It made sense. Maybe they weren't such great horse trainers after all. Maybe this guy was telling the truth.

"Let me tell you what happened," said Luke. "Last night while we was roundin' up a bunch of our horses and herdin' them into the corral, this here rascal got other ideas. Seems last thing he wanted to do was spend the night in a corral with a bunch of other horses. So, what does he do? He takes off running into the desert like a wild banshee. We've been on these horses all night and all day lookin' for this here horse. We was just 'bout ready to give up lookin' when we seen you. Can't tell you how 'bliged we are to you for finding him like you did."

Then, one by one, Karl took them off Beauty.

"Are you sure this is your horse?" Tyler asked as Luke set him down.

"Yeah, are you really, really sure?" asked Sam with her hands on her hips.

"Why, 'course I'm sure. And just to show you how 'preciative we are to you for finding him for us, I'm gonna give each of you a reward."

He took his wallet out his back pocket, reached into it, and took out some money.

"There you go," he said as he gave each one of the kids a five-dollar bill.

Karl got off his horse and put a rope around Beauty's neck and tied her to his horse. It was obvious that Beauty didn't like him very much because she was acting all nervous and trying to back away from him.

"C'mon, Luke," said Karl, grumpily. "We's burning daylight."

"Thank you again, kids," said Luke with a big friendly smile.

And then they both got on their horses and rode off in a cloud of dust.

"'Bye, Beauty," said Sam softly with tear-filled eyes.

The kids stood there for a long time watching those two men ride off with their one and only horse until they disappeared over a hill.

Then all of a sudden, Sam's eyes got real big and she said, "Oh my gosh!"

"What's the matter?" asked Tyler.

"They're lying!" she said.

"What do you mean?" asked Stoney.

"How do you know that?" asked Tyler.

"I just remembered! I saw that guy back at the gas station," said Sam, "the one with the patch over his eye."

"Are you sure?" asked Tyler.

"Yes. And I heard him say 'Don't worry, we know how to *steal* a horse.' And they lied about being on their horses since this morning too, 'cause it was only a little while ago when I saw him at the gas station!"

"Are you sure Sam?" asked Tyler again.

"Yes! I'm sure!"

"We can't let them get away with this. C'mon, we're gonna get our horse back," said Tyler.

Sam and Tyler started walking, but Stoney just stood there.

"Aren't you coming?" asked Tyler.

"No," said Stoney.

"Why not?" asked Tyler.

"Uhhh. . . . 'Cause I gotta get back home. My mom's gonna be wondering where I am."

Tyler knew Stoney was just scared, so he said, "Okay, that's up to you, but be careful of the coyotes and the mountain lions and the rattlesnakes. C'mon, Sam, let's get our horse back,"

Then Tyler and Sam turned and started walking away.

It only took Stoney a couple of seconds, thinking about coyotes and mountain lions and rattlesnakes, before he changed his mind and started running after Tyler and Sam. "Hey, you guys ! Wait for me!"

Chapter 9
Snake Canyon

The kids followed Luke and Karl's tracks up hills and down hills and across a big valley. Then they saw some big, red mountains ahead of them. The tracks were heading right to them.

Just then, Sam spotted something on the ground and picked it up. "Hey! Look at this! What do you think it is?"

When Tyler looked at it, he knew right away what it was. He took it from Sam and shook it. "It's a rattlesnake rattle," he said. Then he handed it back to Sam. "C'mon, let's go."

They kept following the horse's tracks until they finally came to a place right in the middle of the red mountains called Snake Canyon. It was the coolest place they had ever seen. It looked a lot like the surface of the moon. All the rocks and cliffs were red with caves and holes everywhere. And right in the middle of the canyon was this gigantic rock that looked just like the head of a huge snake with its mouth open.

And then a scary thing happened. The tracks led them right into a big cave where Luke and Karl were! The horses were tied up, and Luke and Karl were sitting and talking in front of a fire. It was lucky Luke and Karl didn't look up right then because they would have seen Tyler, Stoney, and Sam for sure. The kids quickly ducked back out of sight.

"Whew! That was close," whispered Sam.

"You can say that again," said Stoney.

"Shhh! Listen!" said Tyler.

They leaned toward the entrance to the cave and listened to Luke and Karl talking.

"So why do they call this here place Snake Canyon?" asked Karl. "'Cause of that big rock out there?"

"I'll tell you why," said Luke. "'Cause there's snakes

everywhere out here! One time, when I was a kid, I climbed up in one of them there holes just to get out of the burnin' sun for a spell, when all of a sudden, this great big rattler fell from up above and landed right in my lap. His head was as big as my fist."

Luke made a fist and held it out for Karl to see.

"What'd you do?" asked Karl, all scared-like.

"I didn't do nothin'. I just sat there, still as could be, 'til that deadly thing crawled off a' me."

"I hate snakes more than anything," said Karl, shuddering, "'cept maybe rats."

Tyler looked over at Stoney, and his eyes seemed as big as some of the holes in the red rock.

They kept listening and learned that there was a third horse thief named Ray. Ray was coming with a big truck to take Beauty to Mexico, where they were gonna sell her for a lot of money. The kids knew they had to act fast before Ray got there. *But what could three kids do against two big men?* Tyler thought to himself. Right then, Tyler looked down at the rattle in Sam's hand and got a great idea.

Chapter 10

Fake Snake

Tyler, Stoney, and Sam looked around Snake Canyon and found a skinny cave that went way back into the rock and finally came out under a small ledge. It was perfect for Tyler's plan.

While Luke and Karl were still sitting by the fire, Stoney ran into the cave and shouted real loud. "Hey, you guys! You stole our horse, and we're gonna call the police!"

It scared Luke and Karl so bad they almost jumped out of their boots.

"Get him!" shouted Luke.

"You get him!" Karl shouted back.

"I said get him!" shouted Luke even louder.

Stoney took off running out of the cave with Karl in hot pursuit.

From a hiding place in one of the rocks, Tyler watched Karl chase Stoney all over Snake Canyon. Just as Karl was about to catch him, Stoney ducked into the long, skinny cave. So far their plan was working. The cave was only about three feet high inside, so Karl and Stoney had to crawl through it on their hands and knees.

"Come back here, kid!" shouted Karl.

Stoney crawled as fast as he could, but Karl was gaining on him. Then, just as Stoney was almost to the end of the cave, Karl reached out and grabbed hold of Stoney's cowboy boot.

"Now I've gotcha!" shouted Karl, laughing.

Stoney screamed, reared back, and kicked Karl hard, right smack in the nose with his other boot.

Karl had no choice but to let go of Stoney. His nose was aching and bleeding. "Kid! You're gonna pay for this!" he shouted.

Stoney scrambled as fast as he could to the end of the cave, slipped out, and ran off.

Getting out of the cave wasn't so easy for Karl. He had to get down on his belly and squeeze through the small opening. When he finally did manage to get out, Sam was waiting on the ledge above him with one of Stoney's ropes. Before Karl could get to his feet,

Sam dropped the coiled rope right on top of his back! *Thump!* When Karl felt the rope, he froze. He was sure a big, deadly rattlesnake had dropped on him.

Sam quickly took the snake rattle out of her coat pocket and started shaking it. Now Karl was *sure* a rattlesnake was on his back. He looked up at the sky and, with tears in his eyes, said pleadingly, "Please, Lord, don't let me die. Just as soon as we sell this horsey, I swear I won't steal no more."

When Sam heard this, she shook the rattle even harder.

While Sam was keeping Karl busy, Tyler and Stoney waited outside the big cave for Luke to go looking for Karl. When he finally did, they ran into the cave and untied The General.

"Come on, Beauty. Let's go," said Tyler, pulling on the rope. But The General didn't budge. Tyler pulled even harder, but he still wouldn't move.

"I don't think she wants to leave the other horses," said Stoney.

Outside in the canyon, Luke was walking all over searching for Karl. "Karl! Karl! Where are you?" he kept shouting. Then, just as he was about to turn around and go back to the cave, he heard Karl whispering. "Luke! Luke! Over here! Luke!"

"Karl? Where are you?" shouted Luke.

When Sam heard Luke's voice, she quickly got up and ran off.

Luke stepped around a big rock and saw Karl lying on his belly under the ledge, crying like a baby with Stoney's rope on his back.

"What are you doing Karl?"

"Shhhh! Snake! There's a snake on my back!" he said, sobbing.

"I see it. Don't move," said Luke.

"What are you gonna do?" whispered Karl.

"Just you hold still and don't move," said Luke.

"Please, don't let him bite me, Luke. I'm too young to die."

Luke slowly walked over to Karl and grabbed the rope, then threw it down right in front of Karl.

"There's your snake, Karl!" shouted Luke.

Karl was confused and stared at the rope for a long time. "That ain't no snake," he said. "That there's a rope."

"That's right!" Luke shouted again. "It's just a rope! You got duped by kids, Karl!"

Karl slowly got to his feet, looked at the rope again, and began scratching his head. "Honest, Luke. I really did hear a snake rattlin' his tail. Honest."

"Yeah, yeah," said Luke. "C'mon, we gotta get back to the horses."

Back at the cave, Tyler and Stoney still couldn't get The General to leave the other horses. Then all of a sudden, they heard Sam yell, "Tyler! Stoney! They're coming! Hurry! Get out of there!"

They looked up toward the back of the cave where there was a small hole that led to the outside. There was Sam looking down through the hole at them. "Hurry!" she shouted again. "Get outta there! They're almost here!"

The boys let go of the rope and started to run out of the cave just as Luke and Karl came walking in.

"Get the cowboy!" shouted Luke. "I'll get the other one!"

Tyler tried to run by Luke, but Luke grabbed him and picked him up off the ground. Tyler tried to wiggle free, but Luke was just too strong.

When Karl tried to grab Stoney, he slipped and fell, which gave Stoney just enough time to run out of the cave.

"Go get him, Karl!" shouted Luke.

"Do I have to?"

"Yes!"

"But, Luke," pleaded Karl, "trying to catch that little cowboy is harder than herding a bunch of jack-rabbits onto a flatbed truck!"

"I said get him!" shouted Luke.

Karl just shrugged his shoulders and ran out of the cave.

As soon as Karl left, Luke tied Tyler's hands behind his back and pushed him to the ground next to the fire. Luke looked at Tyler with his one good eye and said,

"Don't even think 'bout trying to get away, kid, 'cause I got my EYE on you."

Tyler was more scared than he'd ever been in his whole life. He wished then that he had never watched that movie about wild mustangs.

Chapter 11

Sam to the Rescue

Karl chased Stoney up and down and over the rocks. Stoney was getting tired, and it was only a matter of time before Karl was going to catch him. "When I get you, kid, I'm gonna wring your skinny little neck for makin' me run all over tarnation like this!" shouted Karl.

Sam was watching the chase from the top of a big rock when she got a great idea. She grabbed one of Stoney's ropes and hurried off.

Meanwhile, Stoney was jumping like a jackrabbit from one rock to another when suddenly he came to what seemed like a dead end. His only escape was to jump across a nine-foot crevice to another rock. Stoney had never jumped this far before in his life, and if he didn't make it, he'd fall forty feet to the rocks below. He looked back up and saw Karl getting closer. When Karl saw that Stoney was trapped, he smiled really big. "I got you now, kid," he said as he inched closer. "And now I'm gonna wring your little neck!"

"That's what you think!" said Stoney. Stoney took off his hat, backed up, then took off running as fast as he could. When he got to the edge of the cliff, he leaped high into the air and sailed across the ravine, barely making it to the other side. He landed hard, rolled, then quickly got to his feet, put his hat back on, and raced down a narrow path.

"Dang it, kid!" shouted Karl. "Git back here!"

By this time, Sam was hurrying up the trail when she heard Stoney and Karl coming toward her. Time was running out. Looking around frantically, she spotted a big rock by the side of the trail and quickly tied one end of the rope around it. Then, with the other end, she ran across the trail and ducked out of sight behind a big bush. Within seconds, Stoney flew by, huffing and puffing. Sam got ready. She had never done anything like this before and could feel her heart pounding in her chest. She could hear Karl getting closer and closer. "Kid!" she heard him shout. "Slow down! You're killing me!"

Then just as Karl got to the rope, Sam yanked on it with all her strength. The rope tightened. When Karl's foot hit the rope, he tripped and went flying through the air, landing hard on his stomach.

"Yes!" said Sam to herself.

Before Karl had time to look back to see what had tripped him, Sam had already run out from behind the bush, grabbed the rope, and disappeared out of sight.

Karl stumbled to his feet and looked back. He was really confused. He didn't know what to make of it. First it was a rattlin' snake on his back, and now something invisible had tripped him. Brushing himself off, he limped down the trail. Thanks to Sam, Stoney had just enough time to get away.

When Karl got back to the cave, he was dripping with sweat and all out of breath.

"Where's that little cowboy?" asked Luke.

"I don't know," answered Karl. "He just disappeared into thin air."

"Well, get back out there and find him!"

"It ain't no use, Luke. It's like an Easter egg hunt out there! And besides, I'm tired."

"Well then, I guess I'll just have to find him myself," said Luke. "You stay here and keep an eye on that kid. And don't you let him outta yer sight! Understand?"

Stoney and Sam ran around to the back of the cave and looked down at Tyler through the small hole. They could see that he was tied up, but they couldn't call his name because Karl would hear. So Stoney found a little pebble and tossed it into the cave just behind Tyler. When Tyler heard it, he looked up and saw them. He wanted to tell them that Luke was looking for them and to be careful, but he couldn't. All of a sudden, somebody grabbed Stoney and Sam and pulled them away from the hole. Tyler thought for sure Luke had found them.

But lucky for Stoney and Sam, it wasn't Luke. It was Brad! Brad and Andi had followed their tracks all the way to Snake Canyon!

Stoney and Sam told Brad and Andi the whole story how they found Beauty and how the horse thieves took her from them. That's when Andi told them that Beauty's real name was The General and that he belonged to her grandpa.

"Where's Tyler?" asked Brad.

"He's in the cave, and they've got him tied up," cried Sam.

"Tied up!" exclaimed Brad.

"Yeah, look," said Stoney, pointing to the small opening at the back of the cave.

Brad stepped to the small hole and looked down into the cave at Tyler. Tyler looked up at Brad, who shook his head and gave Tyler the same look he gave him when Tyler put dish soap in his orange juice on

April Fool's Day. Tyler felt really bad that he hadn't listened, and he wished that he'd stayed in the jeep like Brad told him to.

Just then, Brad and Andi thought they heard a truck coming. "Maybe that's the sheriff!" said Brad. "C'mon!"

They ran to the edge of a cliff and looked down. A big, white panel truck was slowly making its way up the canyon.

"Let's take a closer look," said Brad to Andi. Then he looked at Sam and Stoney and said, "You two stay right here."

Then he and Andi ran off.

Sam and Stoney watched until they disappeared out of sight. Then Stoney turned and said to Sam, "We didn't tell them about the other bad guy. What if it's him and not the sheriff?"

Sam and Stoney stared at each other for a long moment. Finally Sam said, "C'mon, let's go!"

Brad and Andi ran around to the entrance of the cave, ducked behind a big rock, and looked out as the big truck pulled to a stop and the driver got out. He had a beard and wore a cowboy hat, a long coat, and boots. When Andi saw him, she got really excited.

"That's Ray!"

"Who's Ray?" asked Brad.

"He works for my grandpa! He takes care of all the

horses on the ranch. Grandpa must have told him to come and get The General. C'mon."

She grabbed Brad's hand and pulled him from behind the rock and ran toward Ray. She had no idea that Ray was bad and that he was there to help Luke and Karl take The General to Mexico and sell him.

"Ray! Ray!" shouted Andi. "I'm so glad to see you!"

When Ray saw Andi running toward him, he didn't know what to say. Andi was the last person he wanted to see.

Stoney and Sam ran to the big rock, and peeked out from behind it just in time to see Luke jump out from behind the truck and grab Brad!

"Hey!" yelled Brad. "What are you doing?"

As soon as Andi saw Luke, she shouted, "Ray! HELP! He's one of the men that stole The General!"

Then something happened that surprised Andi: Ray grabbed her and shoved her toward the cave.

"Ray! What are you doing?" shouted Andi. "Let go of me!"

But Ray didn't let her go and wrestled her into the cave.

When Sam and Stoney saw this, they ran to the back of the cave and looked inside again. They watched in horror as Luke, Karl, and Ray tied up Andi and Brad, then shoved them to the ground next to Tyler.

"Now what are we gonna do about them other two little kids out there?" said Karl.

"We ain't gonna do nothin'," said Luke. "What can two little kids do?"

After Sam heard this, she backed away from the hole, slid to the ground, and started to cry. "He's right, Stoney. We're just two little kids. What can *we* do?"

Stoney started walking back and forth thinking real hard. Then he stopped and looked down at Sam. "C'mon," he said. "We can't give up yet. Let's take a look and see what's in that truck. Maybe we'll get an idea."

Chapter 12

The Plan

So what's the plan, Ray?" asked Luke.

"We're gonna load up the stallion in the truck and take him to the border," said Ray. "The buyers are gonna meet us there in the morning with the money."

When Andi heard this she shouted, "No, Ray! You're not gonna get away with this! Grandpa won't let you!"

Ray didn't say anything. He just looked at Andi, wishing she didn't know he was stealing her grandpa's horse.

"You be quiet!" said Karl. "One more word out of you, little miss, and I'll tape your mouth shut."

"Now you're *sure* they're gonna be there with the money?" asked Luke. "'Cause I don't want to be taking no wild goose chase for nothin'."

"I'm sure," said Ray.

Just then Ray's cell phone rang. He looked at the phone to see who it was that was calling. "It's the old man," he said quietly. "I'll be right back."

Outside of the cave, Sam and Stoney were hiding behind a big tumbleweed they had found and were slowly moving toward the truck. But just as they started getting closer to the truck, Ray stepped out of the cave with his cell phone and said, "Hello, this is Ray."

When Sam and Stoney heard Ray, the tumbleweed came to a halt.

"Now what are we gonna do?" whispered Sam.

"Just try not to move," whispered Stoney.

Ray seemed like he had seen the tumbleweed move because he kept staring at it while he talked on the phone.

"Hello, JP," said Ray. "Nope, no sign of them yet. But you can be sure I'll keep on looking. I'll call you soon as I find something out. Okay. Bye."

Ray turned off his phone, stared at the tumbleweed one last time, and then walked back into the cave.

"Whew! That was a close one!" said Sam.

"You can say that again," said Stoney. "C'mon, let's go."

Stoney jumped out from behind the tumbleweed,

hopped up on the truck's running board and grabbed the door handle. "Sam! It's unlocked! C'mon."

He opened the door, and he and Sam crawled in.

"Look, the keys are still in it!" said Stoney.

Sure enough, Ray had left the keys in the ignition.

"Hurry, Stoney! They might come!" said Sam.

Stoney reached under the passenger seat, found something on the floor, and pulled it out. It was a metal box. He lifted it up, put it on the seat, and opened it. Inside were tools, matches, a first aid kit, and some road flares.

Stoney held up one of the flares and said, "Look, Sam!"

"What is it?" asked Sam.

"It's a flare. If your car breaks down at night, you light one of these and put it on the road so people can see you need help."

"What are you gonna do with it?" asked Sam.

"I don't know yet. I'm thinking." Stoney thought real hard for a minute and then said. "I've got an idea!" He grabbed the matches and a handful of flares and said, "C'mon, let's go."

Chapter 13
Duped Again

"All right," said Ray. "It's time to go. Let's load up the horses."

Luke and Karl walked over to the horses and were ready to untie them, when suddenly they heard the truck's horn. It sounded like it was stuck because it just kept on blaring.

Luke looked at Karl and said, "Go see what's going on out there!"

"How come I always gotta be the one who goes?"

"GO!" shouted Luke.

Tyler looked over at Brad and Andi and whispered, "It's Sam and Stoney. Don't worry, they'll save us."

Brad looked over at Andi and rolled his eyes.

"You'll see," said Tyler.

Sam and Stoney were hiding behind the big rock when Karl came out of the cave. He walked over to the truck and looked inside. His eyes bugged out when he saw a big rock, about the size of a football, tied to the steering wheel and pressing down hard on the truck's horn. Karl tried to open the door, but Stoney had taken the keys and locked it. Karl looked around and spotted a big rock, picked it up, and was ready to smash the window when something caught his eye. Thick black smoke was billowing out from behind the truck!

When Karl saw the smoke, he forgot all about breaking the window and ran to see where the smoke was coming from. When he looked inside the back of the truck, he saw two flares burning and smoking. He quickly dropped the rock, climbed into the back of the truck, and started stomping on the flares.

That's when Stoney appeared out of nowhere, climbed up on the tailgate, reached up, grabbed the door, and started pulling it down. But before he could get it all the way down, Karl saw him and panicked. "Hey! Kid! What are you doing?" he shouted. "No! *No! Stop!*"

Karl dove at the door but he was too late. *Bang!* Stoney closed it just in the nick of time and latched it shut.

"Luke! Luke! Help!" Karl shouted as he pounded on the door.

But Luke couldn't hear him because the truck's horn was making too much noise.

Now that Karl was all locked up, it was time to set the next trap. Stoney quickly made a noose with the end of his rope, laid it on the ground under the truck's door, and covered it with dirt. Then, with the other end of the rope, he crawled to the front of the truck and waited.

Inside the cave, everyone could still hear the truck's horn blaring.

"Luke," said Ray, "Go and see what's goin' on out there."

"Don't you worry none," said Luke, walking out of the cave. "I'll take care of this."

Tyler looked over at Brad and whispered, "One down and two to go."

This time Brad didn't roll his eyes or shake his head. He and Andi just looked at each other for a long time.

Luke came out of the cave and heard Karl yelling and banging around inside the back of the truck. He walked to the back of the truck and shouted, "Karl! What are you doin' in there?"

Karl was coughing from all the smoke and yelled, "I'm dying in here, Luke! Git me outta here!"

"You got duped again, didn't you? By two little kids!"

"Jest git me outta here!" shouted Karl.

While all of this was going on, Stoney was on his hands and knees watching everything from under the front of the truck. Just as soon as he saw Luke step into his noose, he yanked on the rope with all his might. The noose tightened around Luke's boots and pulled Luke's feet right out from under him. Down went Luke! When he hit the ground, his head landed right on top of the rock that Karl had dropped, knocking him unconscious! Stoney hurried to Luke and tied him up as fast as he could.

That made two down and only one to go. Now it was Sam's turn to take care of Ray.

Chapter 14

The General Saves the Day!

The only one small enough to crawl through the hole at the back of the cave was Sam. So when Ray wasn't looking, she squeezed through and snuck down the rocks behind Brad, Andi, and Tyler. She was so quiet that they didn't even hear her coming. When Brad felt her hands on his shoulders, it really scared him. "Shhh! Don't worry," whispered Sam in Brad's ear. "I'm here to help."

And then she started untying Brad's hands. Ray looked over a few times when he thought he heard something but every time he did, Sam ducked out of sight behind Brad.

It took Sam a long time to untie Brad. When she finally did, she leaned over Brad's shoulder again and whispered in his ear. "Okay, here's what you're gonna do. When Stoney comes in, I want you to jump up, run across the cave, and punch that guy right in the nose."

"What!" whispered Brad. He couldn't believe what Sam was asking him to do.

"You heard me! We already took care of the other two guys, so now it's your turn to take care of *that* guy."

Then, just like they had planned, Stoney ran into the cave carrying a burning flare in his hand and shouted, "Hey, mister! Catch!"

Stoney threw the flare right at Ray, then turned and ran back out of the cave. Ray dodged the flare, then started stomping on it to put out the fire.

"*Now!*" Sam whispered to Brad.

Brad jumped to his feet, leaped over the fire, ran and grabbed Ray by the shoulder, and spun him around. Winding up his arm like a baseball pitcher, he punched Ray right smack in the jaw—*Ker-pow!*

Ray didn't know what hit him and fell to the ground, unconscious.

"Good work, Brad!" said Sam. "Now! Quick! Tie him up!"

While Brad tied up Ray, Sam untied Andi and Tyler.

"Okay, let's get outta here!" said Brad.

Then something unexpected happened. Luke somehow got free, ran into the cave, and grabbed Andi!

"Brad! Help!" cried Andi.

Everyone turned toward Andi and Luke.

"Let her go!" shouted Brad.

"I'm the one giving orders now, kid," shouted Luke. "Now here's what we're gonna do." He looked right at Brad and said, "You! Untie Ray!"

That's when everyone heard a strange noise. It sounded like a fan when the blades are spinning real fast. *Whrrrrr!* Andi could hear it too. She turned and saw Stoney in the entrance of the cave twirling his lasso over his head. Andi picked up her foot and stomped the heel of her boot right on top of Luke's foot.

"AHHHH!" shouted Luke. Then she elbowed Luke right in the ribs.

"AHHHH!" he cried again.

Just as soon as Andi broke away, Stoney let his lasso fly. It was perfect! It went right over Luke's head and shoulders, then down and around his arms. Stoney yanked real hard on the rope and pulled Luke to the ground. And then the most exciting thing happened. Andi untied The General and yelled, "Get him, Gen!"

The General ran over to where Luke was and reared up on his hind legs almost hitting his head on top of the cave as his hooves slashed the air. It was awesome!

"Call him off! Call him off!" shouted Luke.

Right there and then, Brad tied up Luke. He tied the knots so tight there was no way Luke was gonna get loose again.

When Brad opened the back of the truck, Karl was all limp and black from the smoke. He looked like a burnt marshmallow. Brad had no trouble tying him up.

Brad and Andi rode Luke and Karl's horses while Sam, Stoney, and Tyler rode The General. Ray, Luke, and Karl were tied together in a line and walked behind the horses.

When everyone finally got back to Brad's jeep, JP, the sheriff, and his deputies were waiting for them. The sheriff told Tyler, Stoney, and Sam that they were brave little heroes and thanked them for capturing the horse thieves. Then he arrested Ray, Luke, and Karl and handcuffed them with real handcuffs. The kids had never seen anybody get handcuffed before. It was real exciting.

Chapter 15

A Horse for Christmas!

After the sheriff took the three horse thieves away, everyone went back to JP's ranch for dinner. They had a big roast beef with mashed potatoes and gravy and the yummiest apple pie they had ever tasted for desert.

When everyone finished eating, Andi's grandpa took everyone out on the ranch to see all of his horses. He said there were over five hundred of them!

"Kids," he said. "I can't tell you how much I appreciate what you did for me today. The General is the finest horse I have ever owned, and I probably never would have seen him again if it hadn't been for you three brave kids. So to show you how grateful I am, I'm going to give each of you your own horse."

Tyler, Stoney, and Sam couldn't believe what they were hearing. "Are you serious?" asked Tyler. "Do you really mean it?"

JP smiled really big and said, "I've never been more serious in all my life. Go ahead, pick out a horse. Any one you'd like. And you can keep it here on the ranch as long as you want."

Then he turned to Brad and said, "And that goes for you too, Brad. Merry Christmas, everybody!"

Wow! Tyler couldn't believe it! Finally, a real live horse for Christmas! He had to pinch himself to make sure he wasn't just dreaming.

Brad, Tyler, Stoney, and Sam climbed over the fence and walked around looking at all of the beautiful horses.

First, it was Brad's turn. After looking at a lot of horses, he chose a big, shiny, midnight-black stallion with a long black mane and tail.

After Brad, Sam wasted no time choosing a beautiful, pure-white mare.

Next it was Stoney's turn. He chose a black and white pinto stallion with a white mane and tail.

"What are you gonna call him?" asked Tyler.

"Apache Thunder," said Stoney.

"That's a cool name," said Tyler.

Finally it was Tyler's turn. He looked at the palominos and the pintos and the buckskins and even a pure white stallion. Then, just as he was about to choose a big palomino stallion, something strange happened. He felt something warm and soft on the back of his neck. He turned around and looked up. There in front of him was a big chestnut-colored stallion with a long black mane and tail, four white stockings, and a white star on his forehead. It was as if the big horse was trying to say, "Choose me."

That was all Tyler needed. He turned to JP and said "If it's okay with you, sir, I'll take this one."

JP smiled, nodded, and said, "The big fella's all yours."

"What are you gonna name him, Tyler?" asked Stoney.

Tyler thought for a long moment. "I'm gonna name him Christmas Wish." Then he said with a big smile on his face, "I'll call him 'Big Chris' for short."

Chapter 16
Wild Llamas

Soon Tyler's wild and crazy Christmas vacation was over, and he and Stoney were back in Mrs. Smith's class. "Students," said Mrs. Smith. "Welcome back. I hope you all had a wonderful Christmas vacation. We're going to start learning about South America. Today we're going to watch a film called *The Wild Llamas of Peru.*"

When she said this, Tyler looked over at Stoney and knew right away what he was thinking, because Tyler was thinking the same thing. Just as soon as the bell rang, Tyler asked Mrs. Smith where Peru was and how long it would take to get there!

About the Author

Writer, director, and author Eric Hendershot was born and raised in a small town in Pennsylvania. He taught in the public schools and was the head wrestling coach for seven years at a large high school before moving to Los Angeles to pursue writing full-time. His first film was *Takedown*, a high school wrestling film distributed nationally by Buena Vista. Since *Takedown*, he has written, directed, or produced eighteen feature-length films and four full-length documentaries. His films have aired on ABC, HBO Family, Nickelodeon, Starz, The Disney Channel, VISN Showtime, and VOD. He currently has five films on Netflix. All of his films have aired internationally. *A Horse for Christmas* is his third published novel.